HENRY AND MUDGE

Get the Cold Shivers

Cynthia Rylant   illustrated by Suçie Stevenson

Winners of the Theodor Seuss Geisel Award

THEN REACH FOR THE STARS!

Each child is a rising star in our Ready-to-Read program, gaining confidence as they launch from one reading lev[...]a constellation of engaging, soon-to-be favorite[...]characters to lead the way, we encourage begi[...]enjoy the journey of learning to read.

The Ready-to-Read stories are grouped into fou[...]

PRE-LEVEL ONE ★ RISING STAR R[...]

Stories are shared reading experiences, featuring [...]characters and simple words.

LEVEL ONE ★ STAR READER!

Stories feature easy sight words and words to sou[...]simple plot and dialogue, as well as familiar topic[...]

LEVEL TWO ★ SUPERSTAR READER!

Stories have simple chapters, longer sentences, and high-interest vocabulary words.

LEVEL THREE ★ MEGASTAR READER!

Stories have longer, more complex plots and character development, challenging vocabulary words, and more difficult sentence structure.

Confidence is a big key to learning to read, and whether a child is a Rising Star or a Megastar, this program is designed to help kids feel like stars at **every** reading level. With the help of their favorite characters, every reading star will sparkle and shine as they take pride in their abilities and learn to love reading.

Blast off on this starry adventure . . . a universe of reading awaits!

Henry and Mudge
GET THE
Cold Shivers

The Seventh Book of Their Adventures

Story by Cynthia Rylant

Pictures by Suçie Stevenson

Ready-to-Read

Simon Spotlight
New York London Toronto Sydney

To Jennifer and Karen Stone—CR
For James Walker Stevenson—SS

THE HENRY AND MUDGE BOOKS

First Aladdin Paperbacks Edition, 1994

Text copyright © 1989 by Cynthia Rylant
Illustrations copyright © 1989 by Suçie Stevenson

Simon Spotlight
An imprint of Simon & Schuster Children's Publishing Division
1230 Avenue of the Americas
New York, NY 10020

READY-TO-READ is a registered trademark of Simon & Schuster, Inc.
Also available in a Simon & Schuster Books for Young Readers Edition.

The text of this book was set in 18 point Goudy
The illustrations were rendered in pen-and-ink and watercolor

Printed and bound in the United States of America

30 29 28

The Library of Congress has cataloged the hardcover edition as follows:
Rylant, Cynthia.
Henry and Mudge get the cold shivers: the seventh book of their
adventures / story by Cynthia Rylant; pictures by Suçie Stevenson.
p. cm.
Summary: When Mudge gets sick unexpectedly, Henry does all he
can to make him feel better.
[1. Dogs—Fiction.   2. Sick—Fiction.]   I. Stevenson, Suçie, ill. II. Title.
PZ7.R982Hj   1994
[E]-dc20   93-45588
ISBN 0-689-81014-8 (hc)   0-689-81015-6 (pbk)
ISBN-13: 978-0-689-81015-2 (Aladdin pbk.)
0816 LAK

Contents

The Sick Day

Henry's big dog Mudge
loved Henry's sick days.

When Henry had a sore throat
or a fever
or a bad cough,
he stayed home
from school in bed.

In the morning
Henry's mother brought him
orange Popsicles,
comic books,
and crackers.

Mudge got the crackers.

In the evening
Henry's father brought him
grape Popsicles,
comic books,
and crackers.

Mudge got the crackers again.

Mudge *loved* sick days.

But even though he loved
Henry's sick days,
no one ever thought
that *Mudge* would get sick.

No one ever thought
that Mudge could catch germs.
But he could,
and one day he caught
a lot of them.

When Henry woke up
and jumped out of bed,
Mudge didn't move.
He didn't get up.
He didn't lick Henry's face.

He didn't even shake Henry's hand,
and he always shook Henry's hand
in the morning.

He just looked at Henry
and wagged his tail a little.

Henry and Henry's mother
looked at Mudge and worried.

"Something's wrong," said Henry.

His mother nodded her head.

"Mudge must be sick," said Henry.

His mother nodded her head again.

"Mudge," said Henry, "are you
just wanting some crackers?"

But Mudge didn't want crackers.

Mudge was sick—
and he didn't even *read*
comic books.

The Vet

Henry and Henry's mother
tried to put Mudge in the car
to go to the doctor.
But Mudge was tired.
He didn't want to go.

"Hop in, Mudge,"

said Henry.

Mudge sat down on Henry's foot.

"Hop, Mudge,"
Henry said again.
Mudge yawned and drooled
on Henry's hand.

"Bath time, Mudge," Henry said,
and Mudge hopped right in the car.
They drove to the vet.

Mudge knew the vet—
and he didn't want to see her.
She made him nervous.

When they walked
into her waiting room,
Mudge started to shiver
and shed.

He did this every time
he went to the vet.
He shivered and shed.

He always left a bunch
of dog hair
on her floor.

When it was his turn
to see the vet,
Henry and Henry's mother
had to pull him
like a horse
into the room.

"Hi, Mudge," said the vet.

Mudge shivered.

"Bad day, Mudge?" said the vet.

Mudge shed.

"He's losing all his hair,"
said Henry.
"I know," said the vet.
"I'd better hurry,
or he may be bald
before you can get him home."
Henry's mother laughed.

But Henry couldn't laugh.

He was too worried.

He was too scared.

The vet looked at Mudge's wet eyes.

She listened to
Mudge's shivering chest.

She felt Mudge's
shedding stomach.

Then she rubbed
Mudge's big head.

"I need to check a few things,"
she told Henry.
"Can you wait outside?"
Henry wanted to say no.
Henry wanted to say *no way*.
But Henry said, "All right."

33

He went back to the
waiting room with his mother.
He sat and wondered if Mudge
knew how to say "ah."

He wondered if Mudge
would be okay.

A Big Kiss

"Your dog has a cold,"
the vet told Henry.
"A *cold*?" said Henry.
"I think so," said the vet.

"He has a fever,
his throat is red,
he's very tired,
and he keeps asking me
for some comic books."
This time Henry could laugh.

"You have to let
him rest," said the vet.
Henry nodded.

"And give him his medicine."
Henry nodded again.

"And don't kiss him
until he's better,"
the vet said.
Henry frowned.
"Aw," he said.

When Henry and Henry's mother
and Mudge got home,
Henry fixed a sickbed
for Mudge in the living room.

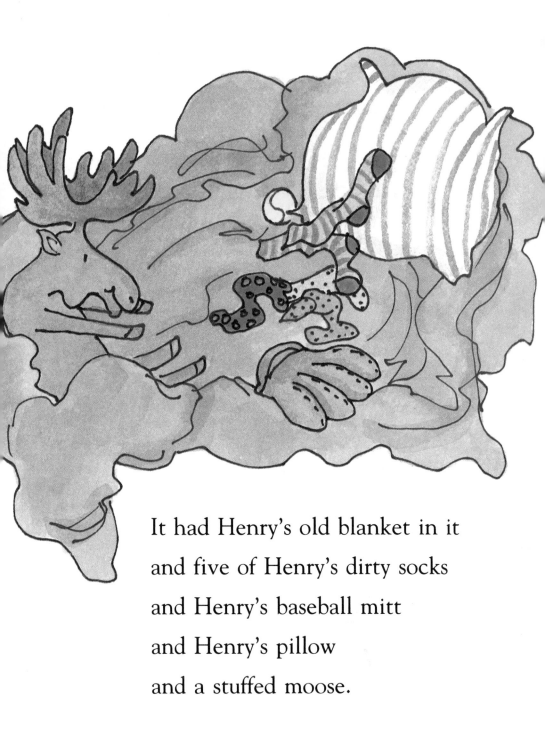

It had Henry's old blanket in it
and five of Henry's dirty socks
and Henry's baseball mitt
and Henry's pillow
and a stuffed moose.

The next morning
Henry brought Mudge
some ice cubes,
a rubber hamburger,
and crackers.

Henry got the crackers.

In the evening
Henry brought Mudge
some ice cubes,
a rubber hot dog,
and crackers.

Henry got the crackers again.

But the next day,

Mudge ate *all* of the crackers.

His sick days were over.

And Henry gave him a great big kiss.